HERGÉ

THE ADVENTURES OF TINTIN

THE BLACK ISLAND

D1530725

Translated by Leslie Lonsdale-Cooper
and Michael Turner

The TINTIN books are published in the following languages :

Afrikaans :		HUMAN & ROUSSEAU, Cape Town.
Arabic :		DAR AL-MAAREF, Cairo.
Basque :		MENSAJERO, Bilbao.
Brazilian :		DISTRIBUIDORA RECORD, Rio de Janeiro.
Breton :		CASTERMAN, Paris.
Catalan :		JUVENTUD, Barcelona.
Chinese :		EPOCH, Taipei.
Danish :		CARLSEN IF, Copenhagen.
Dutch :		CASTERMAN, Dronten.
English :	U.K. :	METHUEN CHILDREN'S BOOKS, London.
	Australia :	REED PUBLISHING AUSTRALIA, Melbourne.
	Canada :	REED PUBLISHING CANADA, Toronto.
	New Zealand :	REED PUBLISHING NEW ZEALAND, Auckland.
	Republic of South Africa :	STRUIK BOOK DISTRIBUTORS, Johannesburg.
	Singapore :	REED PUBLISHING ASIA, Singapore.
	Spain :	EDICIONES DEL PRADO, Madrid.
	Portugal :	EDICIONES DEL PRADO, Madrid.
	U.S.A.	LITTLE BROWN, Boston.
Esperanto :		CASTERMAN, Paris.
Finnish :		OTAVA, Helsinki.
French :		CASTERMAN, Paris-Tournai.
	Spain :	EDICIONES DEL PRADO, Madrid.
	Portugal :	EDICIONES DEL PRADO, Madrid.
Galician :		JUVENTUD, Barcelona.
German :		CARLSEN, Reinbek-Hamburg.
Greek :		ANGLO-HELLENIC, Athens.
Icelandic :		FJÖLVI, Reykjavik.
Indonesian :		INDIRA, Jakarta.
Iranian :		MODERN PRINTING HOUSE, Teheran.
Italian :		GANDUS, Genoa.
Japanese :		FUKUINKAN SHOTEN, Tokyo.
Korean :		UNIVERSAL PUBLICATIONS, Seoul.
Malay :		SHARIKAT UNITED, Pulau Pinang.
Norwegian :		SEMIC, Oslo.
Picard :		CASTERMAN, Paris.
Portuguese :		CENTRO DO LIVRO BRASILEIRO, Lisboa.
Provençal :		CASTERMAN, Paris.
Spanish :		JUVENTUD, Barcelona.
	Argentina :	JUVENTUD ARGENTINA, Buenos Aires.
	Mexico :	MARIN, Mexico.
	Peru :	DISTR. DE LIBROS DEL PACIFICO, Lima.
Serbo-Croatian :		DECJE NOVINE, Gornji Milanovac.
Swedish :		CARLSEN IF, Stockholm.
Welsh :		GWASG Y DREF WEN, Cardiff.

Artwork © 1956 by Éditions Casterman, Paris and Tournai.
© renewed 1984 by Casterman
Library of Congress Catalogue Card Number Afo 20145 and Re 205-198
Text © 1966 by Egmont Children's Books.
First published in Great Britain in 1966.
Published as a paperback in 1972 by Methuen Children's Books Ltd.
Reprinted four times.
Reprinted as a Magnet paperback 1978.
Reprinted nine times.
Reissued 1990 by Mammoth,
an imprint of Egmont Children's Books
Michelin House, 81 Fulham Road, London SW3 6RB
and Auckland, Melbourne, Singapore and Toronto

Reprinted 1991, 1992, 1993 (twice), 1994 (twice), 1995, 1996 (twice), 1997, 1998, 1999, 2001 (twice), 2002.

Printed in Spain by Edelvives
ISBN 0-7497-0469-1

THE BLACK ISLAND

 A plane in trouble?

 Sounds bad.

 It's probably a private aircraft.

 Let's see, Snowy.

 Will it take long to fix?

No, only a few minutes. Nothing seriously wrong.

 Why, it's an unregistered plane.

 Someone coming, Mick.

Too bad for him! You know our orders.

 Are you in trouble? Can I help?

1

Next morning...

Well, doctor? — He was lucky. The bullet only grazed a rib. He'll be up and about in a couple of days.

Excuse me, nurse.

Can we see Tintin, please?

You can go in.

Look here: are you absolutely sure the plane had no registration marks?

Quite certain.

It all looks very fishy to me.

To be precise: the whole thing looks like me, very fishy.

Telephone, please, for Mr Thomson or Mr Thompson.

Hello?...Yes...Interpol?...Yes sir, Thompson, with a p, as in psychology... From Scotland Yard?... Eastdown? Last night?...Yes sir, I understand. We'll leave at once.

We're going back to England. An unregistered plane crashed last night near a place called Eastdown, in Sussex. Goodbye.

Goodbye, and watch your step!

Thanks!

CRASH

?

Why can't you look where you're going?

To be precise: speak for yourself.

Eastdown... If only... It can't be helped, I simply must go. Never mind doctor's orders!

Goodbye, nurse. Many thanks!

Ach! The silly fools! Who d'you think they shot at last night? Tintin himself! — Pity they didn't finish him off while they were about it.

Look!!

KÖLN
BRUXELLES
LONDON

Why have we stopped?

Let's look in the corridor.

There's a door open, and someone's getting out. Come on, Snowy!

There he goes!

What d'you think you're doing?

Eek!

Let me go! A man just jumped off the train. We must follow him!

You can't fool me.

Everybody stay where you are!

No one is to leave the train.

He's coming round.

Tintin! Aren't you in bed?

There he is! I'd know him anywhere. He knocked me out!

Me??

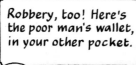

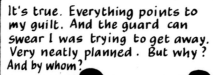

An hour later...

Good! A village. Perhaps I can hire a car to take me to the coast.

CLINK CLINK CLINK

Just wait till I get my hands on him!

To be precise:...er ...just wait till we get our hands!

Hello!

Tintin!

!

You!

Hey, stop!

That's what they call putting your head in the lion's mouth!

Stop him! Stop him!

Where's he gone?

Excuse me, sir. Have you seen a young man running past your house?

Let me see. A young man, you say. That'd be him I saw, with a little white dog. Going like the wind, he was. Hid himself among those trees, over there.

Aha! We've got him!

Snowy!

WOOAH WOOAH

!

Snowy's given the game away!

It's Tintin!

Stop! You're under arrest!

We're gaining on him!

To be precise: we're...

It's your own fault. If you'd kept quiet, none of this would have happened.

Here comes a lorry, going our way. I'll try to thumb a ride.

Lucky for me you're going right to the docks. I'm trying to catch the cross-channel ferry. Think we'll make it?

All right! Haul off the gangway!

So, my friend, we are safely away. Our little plan was a good one, eh?

Not bad at all! By the time Tintin has finished proving his innocence we shall be well clear...

WHEW!

Don't let him see us. We can't do anything here on the boat.

Let's see. We reach Dover in an hour's time. A train from there will get me to Littlegate at ten past five. Then I'll take a taxi to Eastdown from Littlegate station.

Can you drive me to Eastdown?

Yes, sir.

I'm glad to see you, Ivan...No time to explain. Follow that taxi.

Right!

Did you notice that car, Snowy...how it shot past us?

?

It's O.K., they're coming this way ... Ready?

Going to be long, mate?

I...don't know ...It's the brakes ...Something wrong...

!?

Fine!

Too easy!

Look, Puschov; our friend Tintin is coming round.

Aha!

So, you managed to escape from the police. It would have been wiser to stay safely behind bars.

Stop, Ivan. This will do.

O.K.

Get out! And don't try to be clever with me!

Don't you think this joke has gone far enough? What do you want with me?

You needn't put on an act for us. You know as well as we do.

Undo the rope.

Good. Now, my brilliant friend, you are going to become the world high-diving champion. Jump!

All right... Hands up!

Look out! They're coming back!

Let's get out of here!

Don't worry, we'll make sure of him next time.

Come on, Snowy, we must get moving.

You have some brilliant ideas, Snowy. But don't let them run away with you!

Hello... Ja... Doctor Müller speaking... So, it is you... What?... Tintin on our trail... Kruzitürcken! We shall have to keep our eyes open.

Hello, the wreckage of the plane that crashed last night. Come on, let's have a look.

What a mess. What happened to the pilot?

Don't know, sir. We found this lot this morning. No sign of the crew. They must have baled out when they ran into trouble.

It's the plane I saw yesterday. Definitely. But I shan't learn much from this pile of scrap-metal.

Snowy!

Snowy's on to something!

He's picked up a scent; it must be the crew.

There isn't a dog in the world like him. He can smell out a crook a mile away.

Better be on our guard; we must getting close.

Careful...Mustn't take any risks.

Here we go! He's found something.

★!?℮±✳
☀:!⚡
⚡⚡...!⊚

Aren't you ashamed, wasting our time bone-hunting. Here, give it to me.

I've told you dozens of times, you're not to chew filthy old bones.

Here, Snowy! Come here at once!

WOOAH

WOOAH! WOOAH!

!?

Strange...He really does want me to follow him.

I'll come. But woe betide you if it's just another bone.

?

Flying jackets! Those thugs from the plane must have hidden them.

Too much to hope they'd leave anything in the pockets.

Aha! Look there! Some scraps of paper. Something's been torn up. Perhaps this will give us a lead.

I've always liked puzzles, and this time I've got a real one!

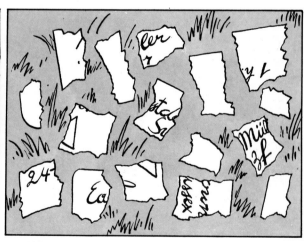

Eastdown
Sussex
Müller
3f. 1.
△
24 - 1h.

Hmm. Not much help. What on earth can it mean? ...

Oh, Snowy, not again!

...and let that be an end of bones for today!

OUCH!

Can't you look what you're doing? ...Anyway, you're trespassing; this is private property.

I'm sorry. I didn't know. I lost my way...

All right, this time. But don't let me catch you again. Take the path down to the river, cross the bridge, and you'll see the main road.

Snowy! Are you trying to make a fool of me?

There's the road.

It must be a couple of miles to Eastdown.

!?

Dʳ J.W. MÜLLER

Here, Snowy! Come here!

We must get out. The dog may have raised the alarm.

YEOW!

A man-trap!

RRRING

Ach so! Someone is caught in trap number nine. Let us take a look.

What a pleasant surprise! Tintin himself, come specially to see me.

Release him, Ivan. He won't run.

Get the car out. We're leaving at once.

It was a mistake to meddle in our affairs. I shall now have to dispose of you. Fortunately, I happen to be medical superintendent of a private mental institution: rather a special institution. Not all of my patients are insane when they are admitted...

...but after eight hours of ... special treatment, they are unlikely to recover. Excuse me: I must make a telephone call then I shall be entire-ly at your service.

I wonder...

Hello, Horncliffe?...I have a young patient for you... highly...er...dangerous. He will require treatment B... You understand? Good!

...a burning log?

Got one... hold it against the rope...

As usual, he seems entirely sane, but...after the treatment...you follow me?

(15)

18

Goodness gracious! I've mixed them up This isn't the key to the station!

So there you are, Fred. How many times have I told you, that's the key to my jam cupboard!

DING DING DING

FIRE BRIGADE

What accursed luck! The fire brigade!

Anyone left inside the house, Doctor?

Fortunately not. We all escaped.

Wooah! Wooah! They must save Tintin! How can I make them understand? Wooah!

I must stop them at all costs, or they'll find him!

They're busy... now for it... no-one will notice me.

Next morning...

...And what happened to Doctor Müller?

I'm afraid my men couldn't catch him. His car was standing just by the house. He hopped in, with his driver, and they went off at top speed. We hadn't a chance.

A pity. I'd give a lot to know ... why were they so anxious to get rid of me? Never mind Perhaps I'll find a clue at the house, to put me on their track again... The fire can't have destroyed everything ...

You're not getting out of bed?

Of course. I feel absolutely all right.

Heavens! There isn't much left of Dr. Müller's house: it's gutted.

I shan't find anything useful here...

Electric cables. What can they be for?

They seem to go on ...

How odd. Where on earth can they lead?

23

CRACK

?

A red beacon. I don't understand...

That isn't all. The wires continue along here.

I say, Tintin, are you going to do this all day?

There's another light here, too.

And now a third one...

The three trees are connected in a triangle...

GOT IT!

Müller
3 f. r. △
24 → 1h.

These are instructions to the pilot in that plane. 3 f. r. △ means three flares, red, in a triangle. A signal!

Meanwhile...

And the worst of it is, another plane is due to deliver tonight. If the lights are not on he will go back without dropping his load. And I am running short of money...

We must return, Ivan. This is the plan. We enter the grounds after dark and light the beacons; the plane drops its load, which we put into the car. By tomorrow morning we can be out of the country. What do you think?

Good idea, chief.

That night...

Himmel! The cables have been pulled up. Someone has discovered our installation.

Look over there, chief. The beacons are alight!

Someone else is waiting for the plane! ... If they drop the load now we are finished! ... We have got to stop them. We must put out those lights. Here, help me to cut the wires.

But ... but chief ... the lights are still burning!

I wonder if they'll come tonight.

RRRRRR
?

O.K. to drop. I can see the lights.

Too late! There is the plane.

One out!

Great snakes - they've dropped something!

Let's see!

Tintin, confound him!

Two away!

Another!
THUMP

That fell quite close. It should be easier to spot than the first one.

I wonder what I'm going to find!

Can I put my hands down now? I won't play any tricks.

Wake up, Tintin!

OHO!

Stupid fool! He trod on the rake and knocked himself out. I'll just take his gun...

Golly, what can I do?

WHAM

Quits!

Out cold!

The most important thing is to truss them up securely!

Necessity is the mother of invention, so they say. If you haven't any rope, use wire...

Now for the sacks. Let's see what they contain...

Great snakes! Banknotes!

Forgers! So that's your game. You'll go to gaol for this!

I'd better set about finding the other two sacks.

There's one...

EEK!

OWW!

They're getting away!

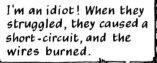

I'm an idiot! When they struggled, they caused a short-circuit, and the wires burned.

Hurry!

The car! They're getting away. Not a hope of stopping them... Unless...

It's my only chance ... If they come this way, it's still possible ...

He'll break his neck!

Aha! ...

Steady now... I must time it precisely ...

Whoops!

Why couldn't he use the gate, like me? ... He always enjoys pretending to be an acrobat... Some people never learn!

28

To let them get away like that - right under my very nose!

Under his nose! They very nearly went over it!

A car! I'll stop it!

PARP PAARP

There's a car just ahead... crooks making a getaway... I simply must go after them...

Crooks?... I say, what a lark!... Hop in the caravan.

We aren't exactly beating the land-speed record! We'll catch them... provided they have a puncture!

The old girl's a bit sluggish; we'll be O.K. when she warms up.

Didn't I say so?... Better already!

Now we're for it!

SPLOSH

Now then, I'm booking you for camping on private property... And in the second place, you've been picking unauthorised fruit... And the third offence, swimming in a manner liable to cause a breach of the peace!

NO BATHING

Oh well, there's no hope of catching them now.

Look, a smash.

Great snakes! It's their car!... Will you drop me here, please?

The occupants?... Not a scratch. I saw them go off towards the railway station...

The train's pulling out!

They're going to catch that train!

He'll go flat on his face again! Just watch!

Come on, Snowy!

I made it – this time!

32

Hello, it's raining.

Golly, that's not water! But it's got a certain something, all the same!

Aha! There must be a leak...

Better try to clean myself up.

STOP!

A station?... No... Then I wonder why they've stopped.

What in the world...? An engine, just sitting there..

It's the one they hijacked. Müller must have abandoned it... But where did they go? The driver may give me a lead ...

Bert! Are you all right? What happened?

A couple of thugs... climbed into the cab... made us drive on ... then ordered me to stop. One of 'em got behind us, clobbered me with a spanner... I went out like a light. Didn't see which way they went ...

That's all right. My dog will pick up their trail in a flash... Snowy!

Now where's he gone?... Snowy!... Hey, Snowy!

SNOWY!

S'O.K., I'm c-c-coming...Give... hic... give a dog a sh-sh-shance...

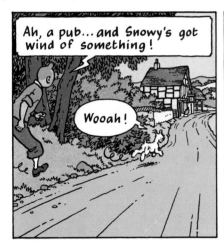

Keep it up, Snowy!

I only hope we're not too late!

HALCHESTER FLYING CLUB

PARKING

Look! Over there! That plane taking off... I bet it's them!

Watch out! He's diving at us!

G·AREI

Ruffians!

To be precise: road-hogs!

G·AREI

Our hats...?

There.

The vandals! Our best hats, almost brand new...a pair of perfect bowlers!

I remember when we bought them, seven years ago...A bowl of perfect purlers!

I'm beginning to agree with Tintin: they look like crooks.

To be precise: so do I. Tintin may be right: they cook like rooks!

RRRR

? ?

Wait for me, I'll be back! Goodbye!

Come on! After them! That other machine over there... Quick!

We're police officers... Start her up... We're taking off right away!

But sir, I...

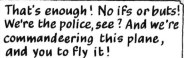
That's enough! No ifs or buts! We're the police, see? And we're commandeering this plane, and you to fly it!

Police... Understand?

Full throttle, pilot!

You can cut out the... er... aerobatics!

I'm s-s-sorry, s-s-sir... I'm d-d-doing my b-best... It's the f-f-first time I've f-f-flown... I'm just the m-m-mechanic!

We'll soon be on their tail, unless...

Just as I feared... Running into cloud...

Rotten visibility... We've lost sight of them.

Have to land... We're near the coast... don't want to drop in the drink.

Doesn't look too rough. I'll have a go...

A wall! We're done for!

38

CRASH CRACK **?**

You all right?

Och, the puir wee laddie! He's fallen inta the brambles.

Come ben the hoose. I'll gi'e ye some mair clothes. It's nae far.

A neer thing...

That's putting it mildly!

Listen, that's the sound of a plane. You won't be able to see it in this mist.

We positively insist. Put us down!

But I keep on telling you: I don't know how to land.

The controls, you idiot! Don't take your hands off the wheel!

Whew! I thought my last hour had come.

To be precise: mine too!

In ye go.

Ye'll find a'ye need i' the other room.

Thanks.

?

A'richt?

Fine! I'm coming down.

There!

OH!

Snowy! Up to your old tricks again!

That certainly seems to be the best solution...

...And let this be a lesson, you drunken, disobedient dog!

Our friend has suggested that we spend the night here. It's getting late.

That's an invitation we'll certainly accept. How very kind of you.

Next morning...

...The dense fog that blanketed the British Isles during the night caused a number of accidents...

Off the Scottish coast this morning, fishermen from Kiltoch discovered floating wreckage of a light aircraft registration G-AREI. There was no trace of the crew, who are presumed drowned.

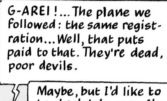

G-AREI!... The plane we followed: the same registration... Well, that puts paid to that. They're dead, poor devils.

Maybe, but I'd like to be absolutely sure. I'm going to Kiltoch ...to look around.

It's no above fifteen miles tae Kiltoch. But mind ye keep tae the path thra' the glen.

Thanks!

Fifteen miles: that's quite a step. We shan't get to Kiltoch before evening.

!?

Snowy! Come here!

Wooah!

Wooah! Wooah!

WOOAAH!

WOOAH! ?

WOOAH!

My poor Snowy!

Whatever made you sit on a thistle?

I can smell the sea. We must be fairly close, now.

Look, there's Kiltoch!

'Evening.

I wonder if you could put me up for the night?

Aye, for sure.

That's fine. I'd like something to eat, too, please... I've just arrived in Kiltoch... and heard about the air crash. Poor fellows. Do you know, have they re-covered the bodies?

No, there's no even a sign o' them yet.

And no more there wull be, neether.

?

?

Nivver!

Why not?...

Why not, ye say?...Ha! Ha! Ha! A'body can see you're no frae these parts, laddie, else ye'd ken for why they'll no be seen agen. Have ye no haird tell o' THE BEAST?

?

The Black Island!

They were quite right in Kiltoch... It is a sinister place...

I think we'll explore the castle first.

That must be the staircase to the tower.

What a marvellous view!

THUMP

THUMP

It's locked!... We're caught in a trap!

Come on, let's find another way out...

THUMP

Too late!

If I can't knock him out this time, we're finished!

RHAAH!

Don't miss, Tintin!

Good heavens! He didn't even feel it!

BONK

What's he doing? He seems to be looking for something...

Crumbs!

RHAAH! RHAAH!

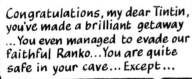

Get back! And put up your hands!

That's enough horseplay. There's a coil of rope over there. You, puss-in-boots, bring it here and tie up your friend with the whiskers. And make a good job of it!

Get a move on! Pull that rope tight, as well. I don't want to have to shoot you.

Your turn now...There, that'll do... It's amazing how quickly thugs come to their senses at the wrong end of a loaded gun.

A loaded gun??...Of all the stupid clods!...I've just remembered: there's no ammunition in my pistol!

A fine time to think of that!

Great snakes! He's right. It's completely empty!

Help! Help!... Rescue!... Help! Help!

Help!... Help! Tintin's here...Help! Help!... Help!

Stop that! Shut up, or I'll...

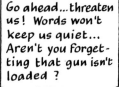

Go ahead...threaten us! Words won't keep us quiet... Aren't you forgetting that gun isn't loaded?

Maybe. But there's more than one way of using an automatic... I'll demonstrate!

Golly, that's the stuff, Tintin!...One!... Two!..Knockout!

Too late! They've raised the alarm... I can hear footsteps... someone coming...

Quick! An ink roller...One of those will be more effective than an empty gun.

No one here!

We're too late, he's gone.

This is Tintin's handiwork, and no mistake! The schwein-hund made off when he heard us coming. Go and warn the boss... And hurry!

My old friends ...Dr Müller ...and his man Ivan!

Ivan!... I ...

THUD

What is it, chief?

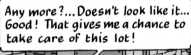

Any more?... Doesn't look like it... Good! That gives me a chance to take care of this lot!

There, that'll do. And be good boys while I'm away!

WOOAAH

Fully loaded: that's better. Still, I hope I shan't need to use it... Now, let's go...

O.K. But mind what you're doing this time!

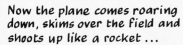

Now the plane comes roaring down, skims over the field and shoots up like a rocket...

Stop! We want to get down, d'you hear?

Now he's heading for the ground again...and into another flawless loop he goes, then... Good heavens! one of the passengers has slipped out of his seat... This is terrible!

Whew! What a stunt! That really had us fooled!

And this time he really is coming down... He's going to land... He's cut the motor...

He touches down... the plane bounces...

...and does one last, hair-raising somersault before it comes to rest in the centre of the field.

A clear victory! The judges are unanimous ...the aerobatic championship is yours!

55

I mustn't waste time... Let's see what else they've got...

A radio transmitter! I'm in luck!

SOS... SOS... Calling the police... Calling the police... This is an emergency... Are you receiving me?...

Police control ... Police control... We are receiving you loud and clear ...Come in please.

It's that secret transmitter... The one we've been hunting for the past three months...

They can hear me!

Tintin calling the police...Tintin calling... I'm on the Black Island, off Kiltoch. I've rounded up a gang of forgers and am holding them here. Can you send a squad to pick them up?... Over!

Police control... Police control... Message received and understood. We will send help at once. Good luck, Tintin!...We'll keep in touch with you... Over and out!

Well, that's that! The police will be here soon, then we'll be able to say goodbye to the Black Island.

About time too. I've had enough of this mediaeval menagerie!

Crumbs! He's managed to free himself!

Now we're for it!...The others will all be loose, as well; we shall have the whole gang after us!

Quietly...Quietly...Here, load your guns. I don't want any mistakes this time!

Don't worry, we'll make him pay for what he did to us!

Sssh!

There!

You go round outside and cut off his retreat.

ZZZING

Got you!

Trapped!

BANG

BANG

He's taken refuge in the tower.

Excellent! We've got him cornered!

Police control... Police control calling Tintin...We are coming to your assistance...A police launch is heading for the Black Island at full speed. Two detectives are with the officers on board... End of message. Over to you... Tintin...Tintin are you receiving me?... Come in, please...

Crumbs! No more ammunition!... I'm done for!

Come on! His gun's empty. Bring him down!

Thank goodness I've still got something...

CRACK CRASH

YOW

OW

There's the Black Island. Only a few minutes and we'll be ashore.

I'm going to fetch Ranko. At least he won't be put off by a few stones...

That seems to have cooled their enthusiasm...

RRR
RRRR

I can hear an engine...

Hooray!... The police!

RRRAH!

WOOAH

Ranko won't be long!

Ready... Steady...

Wait for me! Go!

If you'd done as I said...

Mind the bump!...

Drop your guns! The police! We've had it!

Tintin! You can come out now. It's all right... It's us!

Come on, Snowy, our troubles are over... Down we go!

59

I'm so sorry... I tripped over a stone...

Oh?

Really?

What happened? Did they put up much of a fight?

No, no... To quote Christopher Columbus... er... Captain Cook... er... well, someone about that time: "We came, we saw, we conquered!"

Splendid!... Before we go, I want to have a last look round. Why don't you come with me?

A plane!

But what about an airfield? How did they... er... land?

We shall see. There's a door over there, with a steel shutter.

The beach at low tide... You see? That was their airstrip.

Here's another lot of those sacks, full of forged notes ready for dispatch.

Brrr! It's cold down here. Let's go on up.

Between ourselves, I shan't be sorry to leave this place... I... er... Do you ... er... believe in ghosts?

Me?... Believe in ghosts? Ha! Ha! H...

WOO HOO HOOO

A g-g-ghost!

To be p-p-precise: a s-s-sp-spook!

A ghost?... The castle haunted?... What are they babbling about? ...

WOO-HOO

TINTIN!

T-TINTIN!

It's all right. You can come up now. There's no danger: and no ghost!

It was this poor old chap howling. He broke his arm falling down the tower staircase, just before you arrived. We're the best of friends, now.

W-what are you going to do with him?

Take him with us. If we leave him here the poor beast will starve to death. Far better find him a comfortable home in a zoo.

Come on, let's go. The launch is waiting for us.

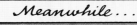

Meanwhile . . .

Aye, sirs, ye can pu' it in your newspapers that they blackguards'd nivver've been ta'en but fer me. A'says tae yon wee laddie, a'says, "Awa' wi' ye. There's somethin' gey queer afoot on yon Black Island," a'says. "And whit aboot yon beast?" says he. "A muckle o' lies," a'says. "Ye'll nae be findin' a beast, nae mair than in this bar." That's whit a'tells him, and he's up and awa'.

They're coming!

Hooray!

Come on!

Good old Tintin!

Welcome back, sir. Can we have a few details? Your own words...

I...er... Well, I ...

How very odd! Did I say something wrong?